Hello Kitty
and friends

The Magazine Mix-Up
·A HELLO KITTY ADVENTURE·

Hello Kitty

and friends

The Magazine Mix-Up

· A HELLO KITTY ADVENTURE ·

HarperCollins *Children's Books*

MEET Hello Kitty

and friends

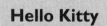

Hello Kitty

Mimmy

Tammy

Mama

Papa

Grandpa

Grandma

Fifi

Dear Daniel

With special thanks to
Linda Chapman and Michelle Misra

First published in Great Britain by HarperCollins *Children's Books* in 2014

www.harpercollins.co.uk
1 3 5 7 9 10 8 6 4 2
ISBN: 978-0-00-754068-6

Printed and bound in England by Clays Ltd, St Ives plc.

MIX
Paper from
responsible sources
FSC™ C007454

FSC™ is a non-profit international organisation established to promote
the responsible management of the world's forests. Products carrying the
FSC label are independently certified to assure consumers that they come
from forests that are managed to meet the social, economic and
ecological needs of present and future generations,
and other controlled sources.

Find out more about HarperCollins and the environment at
www.harpercollins.co.uk/green

Contents

Back to School!

Hello Kitty swivelled around in the chair and waved at Mama and her sister, Mimmy. They were sitting on the side in The Gloss and Gleam Hair Salon, waiting their turn while Hello Kitty had her hair cut. The hairdresser sprayed Hello

Hello Kitty and friends

Kitty's hair with water and then — snip, snip, snip! Hello Kitty couldn't wait to see what she would look like. She was sure her new haircut would be totally **SUPER!**

Hello Kitty was holding a shoe box on her lap. She took a little peek inside; wrapped in tissue paper were a pair of perfect black shoes with little bows on them. They were for school and Hello Kitty LOVED them.

She put the lid back down. She really wanted to try them on again, but Mama had said she had to wait – the start of school was only two days away. Hello Kitty let out a happy sigh. Getting back to school where she got to be with all her friends again – what could be better than that? Fifi, Dear Daniel and Tammy were her very **BEST** friends. Together with Hello Kitty they made up the Friendship Club – they

met after school and in the holidays to do all
sorts of fun things like baking, arts and crafts,
having makeovers – and making up mottos
about friendship. After the hair cut Hello
Kitty was meeting up with them all at the ice-
cream parlour.

Hello Kitty swung back round. The haircut
was nearly finished now! The hairdresser turned
to Mama White and asked if she should cut off
any more. Mama White looked at Hello Kitty
but Hello Kitty said that she thought that it was
short enough – she still wanted to be able to
put her hair bow in it! She always wore a hair
bow on the left hand side of her head and her

The Magazine Mix-Up

twin sister, Mimmy, always wore one on the

right so people could tell them apart.

Mama chuckled and agreed as the

hairdresser spun Hello Kitty back round to dry

her hair. Brightly coloured fish of all shapes and sizes swam around in the fish tank in front of her. There were orange fish that Hello Kitty knew were clown fish, and stripy fish and bright blue fish. But there was also a little black sucker fish. The hairdresser told Hello Kitty that he was called Jaws and that he cleaned the tank!

As the haircut finished Hello Kitty looked in

the mirror, feeling pleased.

Her hair looked just

right! She **jumped**

down from the chair

and the hairdresser let

her choose a sticker.

It was hard to decide,

but eventually Hello Kitty

settled on a pink and purple butterfly. She stuck

it on her dress and waited as

Mimmy took her turn.

Hello Kitty sat down next

to Mama as the hairdresser

Hello Kitty and friends

started to cut Mimmy's hair. **Snip...**
snip... snip...

While she waited, Hello Kitty picked up a

magazine and started to flick through the pages.

She loved reading books but she also loved

looking through magazines about all different

things, like fashion and beauty and travelling.

She liked looking at all the different outfits in the photos and they always had interesting articles too. Just then, Hello Kitty sat up quickly. The magazine had given her an idea! **Hmmm...** She got out her notebook and started to jot some things down, smiling to herself. Mama White asked her what she was doing, but Hello Kitty told her that it was a surprise and that she would tell everyone at the ice-cream parlour!

Mama White smiled. She knew all about

Hello Kitty's surprises – they were always

really good fun.

Mimmy's haircut was soon finished, so

she and Hello Kitty said thank you to the

hairdresser. Mama White paid, and they made their way to the ice-cream parlour. They pushed back the doors and Hello Kitty *rushed* in to greet her friends who were sitting around a large table with a red-and-white tablecloth. Fifi's mother had brought Dear Daniel and Tammy as well as Fifi, but was off to do a bit of shopping now that Mama White had arrived. She waved goodbye.

When she had gone, Mama asked them all what they all wanted. Fifi said that she would like a tutti-frutti surprise, Dear Daniel wanted a banana split, and Tammy settled on a double raspberry ripple cone with sprinkles. Hello Kitty

and Mimmy both wanted the same – chocolate-chip sundaes! Mama White smiled as she ordered the ice creams and they all chattered excitedly.

Hello Kitty was still clutching her notebook, but she waited patiently to hear everyone's news before she started to speak. Eventually, it was her turn and she told them that she had a **brilliant** idea! It had come to her while she was at the hairdresser. She thought that the Friendship Club needed a back-to-school project to work on. Her

Hello Kitty and friends

friends all looked at her eagerly. What was she going to suggest?

Hello Kitty grinned. How about they start their very own magazine? A school magazine. They all **loved** reading magazines; how much fun would it be to actually write one, too?

Hello Kitty held her breath as she

waited to hear what her friends thought of her idea. Would they like it?

She let out her breath with a whoosh and smiled as the

others all started talking at once – they all

thought it was an **amazing**, super idea!

They decided they would all have their own jobs

on the magazine; they would have a meeting

about it to pick which ones. But first things

first... they could see a waiter coming in their direction, carrying a big tray of ice-cream sundaes. The Friendship Club had some eating to do!

The School Magazine

After a mouth-watering ten minutes of

everyone eating their ice creams and tasting

each other's sundaes, Hello Kitty opened up her

notebook. Mimmy had slipped off to another

table with Mama to read her book. She would

have loved to help with the magazine, but she
didn't think she would have time that
term. She had a flute exam at
the end of it and after school
was taken up with practising
for it. But of **course** the
Friendship Club didn't mind!
They were sure that they would
be able to manage
on their own. Dear Daniel
said that he thought that
Hello Kitty should be the
main editor, seeing as it
had been her idea to put

together a magazine in the first place. But she would do her own pages too!

Tammy and Fifi totally agreed. And... How about if Dear Daniel was the sports reporter, seeing as he was really into football and other sports? He could also be the photographer as he knew a lot about that too, as his dad did that for his job! Dear Daniel **grinned** and agreed. What about Fifi? Hmmm... She could be the designer

as she was so good at art and drawing! Fifi
nodded. So that just left Tammy.

Tammy thought hard and
said that she would like to
do a games and puzzles
page. But she'd **also**
like to do a poetry page
as well because she loved
reading and making up poems!

Which one should she choose? Hello Kitty
suggested that perhaps she didn't have to
choose at all! They were both such good ideas,
why didn't she do both? Tammy beamed. It was
all coming together.

28

 The Magazine Mix-Up

The friends decided they would tell their class teacher, Miss Davey, about it at school first thing tomorrow. *Hopefully*, she would think it was a good idea too!

The next day, Hello Kitty stood in the playground with Mimmy. Little butterflies were spinning round in her tummy. She felt so excited

to be starting school again after the holidays!
And she couldn't **wait** to get to spend every
day with her friends again.

She waved Mimmy off and set off down
the corridor. She couldn't help smiling as she
skipped into the familiar classroom and saw her
teacher and all her friends. As Hello Kitty sat

down at her table with Dear Daniel, Tammy

and Fifi, Miss Davey gave them some paper and

explained that she would like each person in

the class to write about something they would

like to achieve before school ended for the

year. As she came around the classroom and

looked over each of their shoulders, it gave the

Hello Kitty *and friends*

Friendship Club the chance they needed to tell Miss Davey about their idea. Miss Davey smiled as she listened. She thought their idea was excellent; nobody had done a school magazine for **ages**. And if the Friendship Club were able to put it together, then she would be happy to photocopy it for them so it could be available to all the students. Hooray!

After that, Hello Kitty couldn't wait for school to finish so they could get to work straightaway! The first thing she wanted to do was to put together an office. All good newspaper and magazine places had an office.

As soon as she got home that afternoon, Hello Kitty **hurried** round getting things ready. The others had checked with their parents if they could come round and would be there soon. Hello Kitty hopped excitedly from foot to foot as she waited for them.

Fifi was the first to be dropped

off, but Dear Daniel arrived not

long after that, and then

Tammy too.

Hello Kitty led them into the

office she had made in the dining

room and pulled out the table. She had decided

it was going to be the main desk for them to

have their magazine meetings, but she had

also got some big cardboard boxes and

chairs for each of them so they could have their

own desks too. Finally, she pulled out a box of

stationery and said that they could all choose

what they wanted for their pages! Inside there

were:

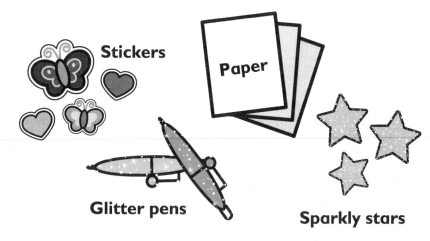

Stickers

Paper

Glitter pens

Sparkly stars

Everyone took what they needed to their

desks. Hello Kitty thought that they should

all spend some time on their own, thinking up

ideas, and then they could meet at the table

to discuss what should go in the magazine. It

would be like a proper newspaper office!

They all nodded, and then the room was

quiet as **everyone** got to work.

Hello Kitty sat at her own desk and chewed

on her pencil as she tried to think of ideas.

She pulled out some of Mama's magazines

to help her. She knew that she wanted to do

something on clothes and fashion, and maybe

a recipe for a home-made lotion or perfume

as well. She looked over at Dear Daniel. He

was *filling* his paper with notes! Tammy

had her head down, equally as busy, and Fifi

was drawing all sorts of things over her pages.

The room was a hive of activity. Hello Kitty

turned back to her own paper just as there

was a knock at the door. It was Mama White

with a big jug of lemonade and some brownies.

Yummy! Hello Kitty poured everyone a

drink and suggested they talk about their ideas while they ate, so Dear Daniel asked her to start first.

Hello Kitty quickly told everyone what she wanted to do. For her clothes and fashion idea, she thought that she would like to do an article on how to jazz up a pair of jeans!

Everyone nodded. It was a very good idea.

Hello Kitty said that she was also going to do a beauty article too. How about they put in

their recipe for Heavenly Hair – the home-made beauty treatment she had made with Fifi and Tammy? It would fit in perfectly!

As everyone smiled, Fifi lifted up her sheet of paper. Because she was the designer for the magazine, she had a logo for the cover. Around where the title of the magazine would be she had put lots of the gold stars. The others all loved it! But what was the title going to be? Oooh... Tammy had an idea. Since they were

Hello Kitty and friends

making it together, and having fun, why didn't they call it **Fun and Friendship?**

Perfect! Everyone grinned at Tammy and patted her on the back. Tammy went pink, and

quickly explained that she'd made a start on her poetry page and puzzles too. Dear Daniel had made a list of all the sports he would like to cover and the games coming up at school. Things were looking **good!** Hello Kitty took a sip of her lemonade. They all had lots of ideas, but what they really needed was something they could do as a main article – something that would be the main piece for the magazine.

The friends all thought hard. Then Fifi **jumped** up. How about they wrote something on the new farm park; Bramble Farm Park? It had just opened not far away and she knew that they were looking to get more people to go. If they wrote a story about it, it might help. Everyone loved animals, didn't they?

That was it! They would ask their parents if they could go and visit it that very weekend. A Friendship Club trip out — what could be better than that?

Bramble Farm Park

Hello Kitty stood with her friends by the

gate at the entrance to Bramble Farm Park and

looked in. There was a big red tractor off to

the side and an arrow pointing straight ahead

to show them where to go. Hello Kitty peered

into a feeding barn where goats and sheep were in pens, surrounded by bales of hay. As the Friendship Club went through the entrance, Mama White told them that it had already been arranged with the owners of the park for Hello Kitty and her friends to be shown around and make notes for their article. Dear Daniel had **even** brought his camera so they would have lots of photos!

Mama bought each of them a little brown bag so they could feed the animals. They were full of little green pellets, and didn't look

all that tasty, but the animals must like them!

Once inside, a guide came over to show

them around. Mama White would meet them

again by the exit at the end. Hello Kitty couldn't

wait to get started!

The guide led them around the farm, pointing out all of the different farm animals that were there and explaining that they were adding to the animals all the time.

First they came to the pigs. Dear Daniel especially liked the pot-bellied ones! They were small and black and **very** sweet. The

guide said that they could feed them, but they

had to hold their hands out flat. Hello

Kitty giggled as they snuffled

over the green pellets in one

quick mouthful and made little

grunting noises. They would be seeing the pigs

again later at the pig races; how exciting!

Tammy loved the smaller petting corner

where children were allowed to stroke bunnies

and guinea pigs. Then they came on to the

goats and sheep. Fifi really liked the miniature donkeys there with them. They had such big fluffy ears and large dark eyes!

Hello Kitty **loved** every minute of it. Her pencil was flying across the page as she took notes; there was so much to write down!

It would all make for a brilliant article. The guide led them on and told them that, over in the trees, there were two more unusual animals which were new to the farm. Hello Kitty could see by the number of people crowded around them that they must be pretty special.

It was darker over in the trees but she could just make out two little pairs of eyes. **Oooh...** She let out a little gasp. Inside was the sweetest pair of reindeer! Their guide explained that it was unusual

to see reindeer in this country so it really was

extra special.

All too soon the tour came to an end and

they were back out in the farmyard. There was

a duck pond to one side where a mother duck

was swimming with her ducklings. On the other

side, the red tractor was giving rides around

the farm park to see the bull and donkeys

and ponies in the fields. There was also a

playground with tyres and swings and slides.

But *luckily*, they were just in time for

the pig race! Their guide pointed over to an

open green shed with a paddock and a little

track in it and suggested they go to watch.

Hello Kitty and her friends raced over. They

didn't want to miss the **race!**

They sat down on the grass. Hello Kitty

looked at the names on each of the pigs'

doors – Squeaker, Pinky, Rocky and Tiny –

Tiny was the littlest one. Hello Kitty decided

that she wanted him to win, and each of the

others chose a pig too. The next thing they

knew, the doors opened and the pigs came

charging out of the shed and went racing

down the track! It was all over very quickly with

Rocky diving, snout first, into the trough of food

that was waiting at the end. They all clapped and Dear Daniel cheered as he took lots of photos – he had picked Rocky to win.

Hello Kitty grinned; it had been so funny watching the pigs snort and squeal their way

down the track. She turned to her friends.

There was **just** enough time for them to

have a play in the playground before they met

Mama White by the exit to take them home!

Hello Kitty made a couple more notes in her

notebook as the others ran to the playground.

Tammy jumped on the monkey bars, Dear

 The Magazine Mix-Up

Daniel slid down the slide and Fifi got on to a swing. Hello Kitty shut her notebook. She would type everything up when she got home but right now, she wanted to join in the fun!

Busy, busy, busy...

Hello Kitty stared at the computer screen

and *sighed*. It was the next day – Sunday

– and the Friendship Club had met up to start

putting everything together for the magazine.

They were going to work on the farm park

article first. Hello Kitty was typing it up, Dear

Daniel was printing off the photos he had taken

and Fifi was finishing some animal doodles

she had drawn to decorate it. Then she was

going to help Dear Daniel choose the **best**

photos. There wasn't anything else to do for

the article, so Tammy was making a start on

her puzzle and poetry pages. Hello Kitty had the most to do — she was typing up the article on the park, and then she **still** had to do the article on the jeans and the hair treatment too.

Dear Daniel, Fifi and Tammy were working busily. Hello Kitty read the three lines she had

so far. Typing felt like really hard work – even with some of Mama's home-made cookies to keep her going!

At that moment the doorbell *rang*. It was Fifi's mother, who had come to collect her. She had an ice-skating practice, which reminded Tammy that she had a music lesson to get to as well. Fifi hadn't quite finished picking all of the

farm photos for the article,
so Hello Kitty and Dear
Daniel would have to
do it. But it couldn't be
helped! Hello Kitty waved
goodbye to Tammy and Fifi and quickly got
back down to work again.

She had **just** finished typing up the article
when Dear Daniel stood
up. He went a little bit
pink as he spoke,
but explained that
he had to go to
football practice as

well. He didn't want to leave Hello Kitty doing

everything on her own, but there

would be plenty of time in the

week for them all to finish

it, wouldn't there?

Hello Kitty took a deep

breath, **smiled** and

said OK. If he had to go,

he had to go! She could do

it on her own. All the same,

she couldn't help but wish the others

were still there. The Friendship Club were

supposed to be doing the magazine together

and now she was going to be the only one left!

As the door closed behind Dear Daniel, Hello Kitty let out a little sigh. Making the magazine wasn't as much fun as she'd hoped. The fun bit had been coming up with the ideas and then being at the farm park! Putting it together and doing the typing wasn't very exciting *at all*. Oh well! She reminded herself that it would all be worth it when it was finished and they had a brilliant magazine to show for it.

Hello Kitty looked at the photos and tried to work out which ones should go in the article. She wished her friends were there so she could ask what they thought though.

After another hour, Mama White came

in and said she thought Hello Kitty needed a

break. She had been working so **hard!**

Why didn't she just print off what she had done

and take it in to show the others the next day?

Hello Kitty nodded. She knew Mama was right. She would just finish this bit and then she was **done.**

The next morning at school, Hello Kitty proudly spread the article out on the table. She

had stuck all the photos in place, and put the
heading that Fifi had designed across the top. It
was looking *really* good.

The others were very impressed. They all felt
sorry for leaving her and gave her a big group
hug to thank her for doing it on her own! They
promised that they would get on with their

articles at lunchtime so that they were ready

for that afternoon. Hello Kitty blushed. She was

very excited about seeing their articles,

and it was going to be so much fun putting them

 The Magazine Mix-Up

all together. She couldn't wait to see what the

finished magazine was going to look like!

A Surprise Solution

After school that day, Hello Kitty and her

friends stood together and looked down at the

magazine. Everyone had written their articles,

just as they had promised. The magazine

was looking good, but still... Hello Kitty thought

that it needed something

more. But what was it?

She flicked through the

pages. There was the

jeans makeover and

the recipe for the hair

treatment and all Fifi's

doodles and designs.

Tammy had finished the

puzzles and poetry pages, and Dear Daniel had

typed up an article on sports. **Right** at the

centre was the article on the farm park – that

looked brilliant with all of the pictures. But why

didn't it look quite right?

Hello Kitty fanned the pages out again and then she realised what it was. It just wasn't thick **enough!** What did the others think? Tammy thought that it looked great as it was. But Fifi and Dear Daniel agreed with Hello Kitty. Still, there wasn't really time to do

anything about it. The magazine had to be in by tomorrow so Miss Davey would have enough time to photocopy it to pass around the school. It would have to do!

At that moment, there was a knock at the door. Hello Kitty turned to see Mama standing in the doorway. Her elbow caught the edge of a glass of water that was sitting on the tabletop. It was as though everything then happened in $slow$ motion. The glass of

water fell, and Hello Kitty spun round to catch

it — but it was a moment too late.

Disaster! Water spilled all over the magazine.

Oh no! What had she gone and done? It was

all her fault — the magazine was ruined! And

after all of their hard work!

Quick as a flash, Mama grabbed the

magazine and brushed the water

off but it was completely soaked

through. It **really** was ruined.

Hello Kitty felt really upset.

What could they do? They'd

just have to tell Miss Davey that

they hadn't been

able to do the magazine

after all. She'd worked

so hard – they all had

– it wasn't fair. Tammy

looked like she was going to

cry and Fifi slumped down in a chair.

Dear Daniel took a deep breath and stepped forward. They couldn't give up now! Not after all the effort they had put in. They would just have to work **extra** hard and do it all over again. It shouldn't be that difficult – they had the articles on the farm park, the jeans makeover and his sports' page all on the computer. They could print those off again, and he was sure that Fifi and Tammy could write out the puzzles and poetry page, and do the doodles and designs again, couldn't they? Fifi and Tammy nodded. They would work as hard as they could to get it done.

Hello Kitty was almost in tears; they just didn't have time. Their parents were about to collect them at any **moment.** Mama put her arms around her daughter and whispered that she thought she might have an idea. How about they turn the evening into a magazine

sleepover? She knew that it was a school night but if the other mums and dads agreed, they could all stay over and work to get it done before they went to bed. Mama White thought she *might* be able to persuade the parents – just this once – that it would be OK.

Hello Kitty gave her a small smile, and Mama quickly disappeared off to phone them.

Hello Kitty and friends

Once she had left the room, the Friendship Club got **straight** to work. There wasn't a moment to waste! Dear Daniel and Hello Kitty ran to the computer and Fifi started drawing

again. Suddenly, Tammy gasped. Mama White's idea of the magazine sleepover had just given her an idea. They had thought the magazine was looking a bit thin. So how about they added another article? A big sleepover article on how to have different types of stylish sleepover! That would make it look thicker. *Fantastic!* The others all loved her idea.

Fifi jumped in; they could put in sleepover games that people might like to play. Dear Daniel said that they could add a list of films to

watch for different types of sleepovers! Tammy

offered to write down some of the stories

she had made up for their sleepovers in the

past, and she also could also write a list of her

favourite books about sleepovers. And

Hello Kitty came up with the idea of designing

some sleepover arts and crafts activities – like

decorating a photo frame or a pencil holder.

There was so much they could write! And of course they also had to have an article on ways to decorate your bedroom for a sleepover too!

They all set to work. They were so busy that they nearly didn't hear Mama White come back into the room. She had a big smile on her face as she told them that all of their parents had agreed and had said they would bring round everyone's nightclothes and  toothbrushes. Hooray! The Friendship Club let out a loud cheer. They told Mama White

about the extra articles they were putting into

the magazine. Mama **smiled** and suggested

that they add a page on sleepover

snacks too. And sleepover music

to listen to, Mimmy chipped in behind

her! She wouldn't mind helping with that –
and with anything else that needed doing.

Hello Kitty smiled. Now that
the magazine would have lots
more articles in it,
it would be even
BETTER
than it had been
before. She couldn't
believe it, but she
actually felt glad the
first copy had been spoiled! Mama smiled again
and told them all it reminded her of one of her
favourite sayings: every cloud has a silver lining!

Hello Kitty *and friends*

All too soon, it was bedtime. Hello Kitty
snuggled down under her duvet while the
others settled all around her in their sleeping
bags. The finished magazine was on the table,

ready for tomorrow. Hello Kitty sighed. She could sleep happily now that she knew the magazine could be given to Miss Davey the very next day. But now it was time to turn the light out and listen to one of Tammy's brilliant bedtime stories!

Fun and Friendship

At school the next morning, Miss Davey smiled widely as she thumbed her way through the finished magazine. She thought it was **wonderful**. How had they managed to think of it all? She loved all the articles – especially

the one on customising your jeans, and the puzzle page looked great. And the article on Bramble Farm Park was **lovely!** It was sure to create lots of publicity for the farm so that they would have more visitors and be able to look after more animals. The sports page and the poetry page were wonderful too, but most of all she LOVED the articles on sleepovers. Sleepovers had been her favourite thing to do with her friends when she was a child. The Friendship Club all beamed with pride. How *SUPER* was that!

Miss Davey announced that she was going

to rush off and run it through the photocopier,

so that they could pass it around the school as

soon as possible. She couldn't wait to show

it to everyone!

Tammy, Fifi, Dear Daniel and Hello Kitty

could hardly sit still in class that afternoon.

The magazine had been given out

just before lunchtime and it

was all that everyone in

school was talking about

– how brilliant it was

and how much fun it must have been to make! Everywhere that Hello Kitty looked, people seemed to be reading it and talking about having their own sleepovers and going to the farm park. All of the Friendship Club's work had been worth it! Hello Kitty turned to her friends. Who would have thought they could have done it? And that it would all turn out all right in the end! She grinned.

Dear Daniel grinned back at her. All the hard work had **DEFINITELY** been worth it.

Tammy linked arms with Fifi and they ran out into the playground. Dear Daniel gave a quick wave to Hello Kitty and then went to join them.

As they played outside in the sun, Hello Kitty looked across at her friends. She realised it was about time for another Friendship Club motto, and she had just thought of the perfect one –

Good Friends Make Even Hard Work Fun.

Hello Kitty and friends

It was just right, and she couldn't wait to tell the others! Smiling happily, Hello Kitty followed her friends out into the sun.

The end

Turn over the page for activities and
fun things that you can do with your
friends – just like Hello Kitty!

Are you ready to be a reporter?

Hello Kitty and her friends loved writing their own magazine, and it's easy for you to do too! Take a look at the following pages to start your own fantastic magazine for friends and family to read.

You will need:

- Paper
- Scissors
- Glue
- Pens and pencils
- Magazines for cutting up – make sure you ask permission first!
- Materials for decorating it – glitter, sequins etc.

MAKE SURE YOU ASK MAMA OR PAPA TO HELP!

What to write about?

Choose something you love - are you into fashion? Sports? Animals? Or is there something you want other people to hear about? You can write about anything you like!

Pick a title?

Your title should tell your reader what your magazine is about and make them want to read it. Choose exciting, fun sounding words; here are some of Hello Kitty's ideas!

Fantastic Fashion

Sports Snap!

Pet Parade

Picture This!

Your magazine needs pictures! You can draw your own, cut them out of magazines or newspapers, or if you have a camera you can even take your own pictures! Try to have at least one picture for each article you've written – you can add more if you want.

Write on

Try to have at least five different articles in your magazine, but they should all be about your topic. For example, in *Hello Kitty's Pet Parade* you can read about:

- *Wonderful walks for you and your dog*
- *How to make your pet pretty*
- *Why Hello Kitty loves pets...*
  And lots more!

Design it

Now you have to decide what your magazine will look like! Choose your colours; they should be eye-catching. If it's about sports, what about your team colours? Or maybe your favourite – Hello Kitty loves pink! You'll also need your title to stand out – look at other magazines for ideas to design yours. You can decorate it with glitter or sequins to really give it some sparkle!

Copy Crazy

When you've finished your magazine, see if a grown-up will make some copies for you, so everyone can read your magnificent magazine!

Jean Genius!

Hello Kitty loves to be stylish, and one of her favourite things to do to stay in style, is to refresh her old clothes! All you need is some imagination and some basic materials and you can turn drab into fab... Follow the instructions to turn a pair of your old jeans into a brand new style – made by you!

You will need:

- A pair of jeans
- Scissors
- Fabric Glue
- Fabric paints and brushes
- Glitter
- Sequins, ribbons, lace, jewels – and anything else you want to jazz up your jeans!

MAKE SURE YOU ASK MAMA OR PAPA TO HELP!

Super Sparkles!

Spread a thin layer of glue in patches over your jeans, and sprinkle them with glitter. Leave them to dry and shake off any excess. Super!

Polka Paint

Using a small brush and fabric paints, paint lots of pretty multi-coloured dots around the edges of your pockets.

Super Shorts!

Cut the legs of your jeans off to make shorts! You can let the cut off legs just fray, or you can glue pretty ribbon around the bottom to decorate them. Ask a grown-up to sew a hem for you if you want to be really neat!

Luxe Lace

Glue lace around the edges of your front pockets, and then glue small jewels along the top of the lace. You'll have the most luxurious jeans around...

Hello Kitty Tip

Make sure all your glue or paint is dry before you wear or wash your jeans. And always wash them inside out to keep your hard work looking brand new!

Turn the page for a sneak peek at

and friends'

next adventure...

The Cupcake Mystery

Hello Kitty huffed on the window and rubbed it clear to look outside. She took a look at all the beautiful orange and yellow leaves on the trees and breathed in happily. She loved the autumn! Her twin sister, Mimmy, was sitting next to her, stringing beads for a necklace and listening to the birds twittering in the trees. For once, they had no friends round to play. It was just the two of them on a clear and crisp Saturday afternoon.

Suddenly someone tickled Hello Kitty's shoulder. She squealed and turned round. Papa was grinning down at her with a bag of recycling in one hand. It seemed like he was the only one doing any work that day!

Hello Kitty and Mimmy both offered to help him but he said he was only teasing. He was enjoying sorting out the house, tidying up all the old papers and magazines and the clothes that they had grown out of. He was going to put all the bags in the shed for now.

He went out the door and down the garden path. Mimmy showed Hello Kitty the necklace she had finished. It was long enough to wear now, and it was beautiful! She smiled as she said that Hello Kitty could have it, and she would make another for herself. Hello Kitty grinned back as Mimmy fastened it around Hello Kitty's neck…

CRASH!

They both jumped and looked round as they heard the sound of breaking glass from the shed.

Papa came out of the door looking
fed up. Oh dear. He'd been moving some
things around and accidentally broken
the shed window. He told the girls not to
go near the shed while he cleared up the
glass.

Poor Papa!

Hello Kitty helped Mimmy make
another necklace for herself. Now what
should they do?

Mimmy said she felt like baking, and
that gave Hello Kitty a super idea. In
the morning they were going with their

friend, Dear Daniel, to visit his granny.
She was feeling a bit sad because her old
dog had been re-homed a few weeks ago.
She had been finding it hard to look after
him as she couldn't walk him every day
any more. So they had decided to go and
see if they could cheer her up. Why didn't
they make some lovely cakes for her?

Mimmy thought it was definitely a
super idea!

They ran into the kitchen. Mama was
there tidying things away, as she had been
making some cupcakes of her own. They
each had one of them with a big glass of

milk, and then they took one out to poor Papa who was still tidying up the glass in the garden...

Find out what happens next in...

Coming soon!

Hello Kitty
and friends

The Cupcake Mystery
·A HELLO KITTY ADVENTURE·

Coming soon!

Hello Kitty and friends
The Cupcake Mystery
·A HELLO KITTY ADVENTURE·

Hello Kitty and friends
The TV Star
·A HELLO KITTY ADVENTURE·

Hello Kitty and friends
The Big Race
·A HELLO KITTY ADVENTURE·

Hello Kitty and friends
The Makeover Party
·A HELLO KITTY ADVENTURE·

Hello Kitty and friends
The Animal Adventure
·A HELLO KITTY ADVENTURE·

Hello Kitty and friends
The Halloween Parade
·A HELLO KITTY ADVENTURE·

Hello Kitty and friends
The Magazine Mix-Up
·A HELLO KITTY ADVENTURE·

Collect all of the Hello Kitty and Friends Stories!

HELLO KITTY and friends
The Friendship Club

HELLO KITTY and friends
The School Trip

·A HELLO KITTY STORY·
HELLO KITTY and friends
The Summer Fair

HELLO KITTY and friends
The Pop Princess

·A HELLO KITTY CHRISTMAS SPECIAL·
HELLO KITTY and friends
The Christmas Present
TWO SPECIAL CHRISTMAS STORIES

·A HELLO KITTY STORY·
HELLO KITTY and friends
The Wedding Day

HELLO KITTY and friends
The Beach Holiday

HELLO KITTY and friends
The Treasure Hunt

·A HELLO KITTY STORY·
HELLO KITTY and friends
The Talent Show

Christmas Special:
Two Stories in One!